Originally published in Dutch as *Kaat heeft een droom* in the series
"De Lettertuin," copyright © 2001 by Bakermat Uitgevers,
Mechelen, Belgium. All rights reserved.

Published in the U.S. in 2002 by Big Tent Entertainment,
216 West 18th Street, New York, New York 10011.

ISBN: 1-59226-047-0

Printed in China.

Listening to Stories

By
Simone Kramer

Kate Has a Dream

Illustrated by
Gudrun Makelberge

BIG TENT ENTERTAINMENT

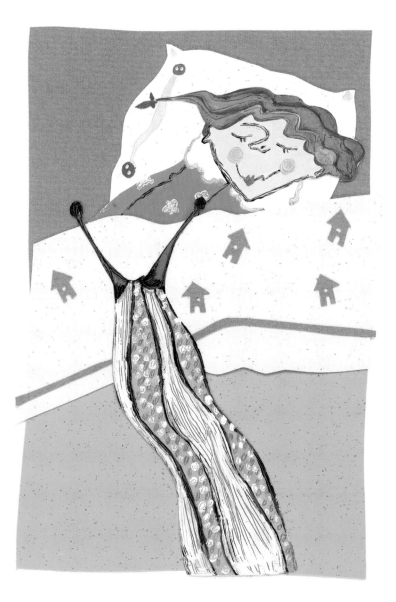

It is night.
Kate is in bed.
She is dreaming.
In the dream
there is a snail.

"Hi, snail. I am Kate,"
says Kate.

"Hi, Kate," says the snail.
"I am looking for my house.
Is this it?"

"No," says Kate.
"This is a bed,
not a house."

"Oh," the snail sighs.
"I will keep looking.
Good-bye, Kate."

"Good-bye, snail."

Kate's dream is not over yet.
Next there is a mouse.

"Hi, mouse. I am Kate,"
says Kate.

"Hi, Kate," says the mouse.
"Do you have any cheese?"

Kate thinks.
Does she have any cheese
in her dream?
No.

What *does* Kate
have in her dream?
"I have oatmeal," she says.
"And ice cream, and a pear,
and a plum."

"Stop!" says the mouse.
"I do not want oatmeal,
or ice cream, or a pear,
or a plum.
I want cheese."

"I am sorry," says Kate.
"No cheese."

"Then I must go,"
says the mouse.
"Good-bye, Kate."

"Good-bye, mouse."

Along comes a chicken.

"Hi, chicken. I am Kate,"
says Kate.

"Hi, Kate," says the chicken.
"Do you know what I can do?
I can lay an egg.
An egg just for you.
Would you like that?"

"No," says Kate.
"I do not like eggs."

"You do not like eggs?"
asks the chicken.
"Cluck, cluck!
Cluck, cluck, cluck,
cluck, cluck, cluck, cluck,
cluck, cluck, cluck...."

The chicken is gone.
But Kate's dream is not over.
Here comes a cat!

"Hi, cat. I am Kate,"
says Kate.

"Hi, Kate," says the cat.
"Is there a mouse here?"

"No," says Kate.
"There was a mouse,
but he is gone."

"Gone?" cries the cat.
The cat is mad.
She scratches Kate's nose
with her paw.

"Ouch!" says Kate.
"Shoo, cat. Get away.
Get away from my dream."

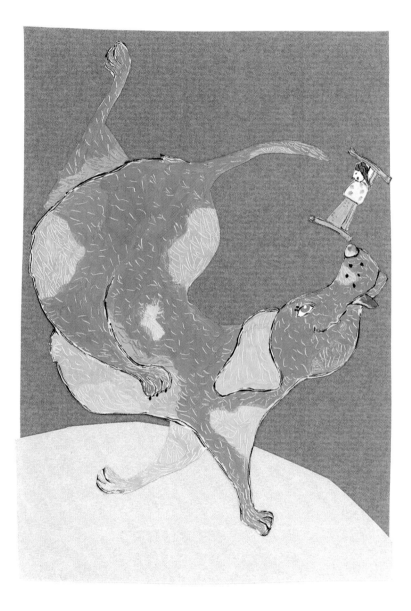

It is still night.
Kate's dream goes on.
She sees a big brown dog.

"Hi, dog. I am Kate,"
says Kate.

"Hi, Kate," says the dog.
"Look at me!
I run very fast.
I run and I jump and I bark—
woof, woof!"

"Kate, will you pet me?"
asks the dog.

"Only if you are quiet,"
says Kate.
"Only if you stop running
and jumping and barking."

The dog is quiet.
Kate pets him.

"Thank you," he says.
"Good-bye, Kate."

"Good-bye, dog."

What is this?
A strange animal
walks into Kate's dream.

"Hi. I am Kate,"
says Kate.
"What are you?"

The animal smiles.
"Guess."

Kate looks at the animal.
It is not a snail or a mouse.
It is not a chicken
or a cat or a dog.
It is not any animal
Kate knows.

"I do not know what you are,"
says Kate.

"Then I will not tell you,"
says the animal.
"Ha, ha, ha!
Good-bye, Kate."

Kate is mad.
She does not say good-bye.

A fish swims into Kate's dream.
A giant fish
with sharp teeth!

"Hi, Kate," says the fish.
How does he know her name?

"Hi, fish," says Kate.
She shivers.
She is cold and afraid.

"Fish," says Kate,
"I am afraid of you."

"There's no need to be afraid,"
says the fish.
"I like you."

Kate is quiet.
She sees the fish's belly.
It looks smooth and soft.

"Will you come
with me to the sea?"
asks the fish.

Kate loves the sea.
"Okay," she says.

The fish and Kate go out to sea.
The sea is nice and warm.

Kate swims low.
She swims high.
The fish is beside her.
They go around and around.

"Climb on my back,"
says the fish.
Kate likes that.
She takes a trip
on the back of the fish.
They go a long way.

The sea changes
from dark to light.
"Look, fish," says Kate.
"It is morning.
I must get home,
and go to school.
But when it is night,
will you be in my dream again?"

The fish smiles
and swims away.